MW00436431

The Wild Upriver
and other stories

The Wild Upriver
and other stories

James McVey

Arbutus Press
Traverse City, Michigan

The Wild Upriver and other stories

Copyright © 2005 Arbutus Press

All rights reserved. No part of this book may be reproduced or transmitted by any means, electronic or mechanical, including photocopying and recording, or by any information storage and retrieval system, except as may be expressly permitted by the publisher. Requests for permission should be made in writing to Arbutus Press, 2364 Pinehurst Trail, Traverse City, Michigan 49686.

Arbutus Press
www.Arbutuspress.com
editor@Arbutuspress.com

Printed in the United States of America

Library of Congress Cataloging-in-Publication Data

McVey, James, 1958-
  The Wild Upriver and other stories/ by James McVey.
    p. cm.
    ISBN 0-9766104-0-X
    1. Michigan–Social life and customs–Fiction. 2. Michigan, Lake, Region–Fiction.I. Title.

PS3613,C83W55 2005
813' . 6–dc22

Cover painting, *Out There,* by David Grath, P. O. Box 272, Northport, MI, 49670
From the collection of Mathew Galvez and Linda Porter

for my family

from the wildflower dunes,
to the islands in the bay

CONTENTS

Going along the north shore of Crystal Lake is pleasant enough in the summertime, with the lake on one side and a steep pine bluff on the other. The water is azure and glitters in the afternoon sun.

A road turns off to the north and climbs through a meadow vivid with hoary puccoons, star thistle, and Queen Anne's lace. At the top of the hill, miles of land and water and sky can be seen at once. To the east is Big Platte Lake, its turquoise color surrounded by the green shades of forests. To the northeast is the bay, rimmed by the tracts of dune country that stretch along the coast. And at the far end of the bay, out across blue Lake Michigan, the majestic bluff of Sleeping Bear dune rises above it all.

The view is lost going downhill as the road enters the shadows of a deep hardwood forest. A few miles further, the road straightens out near Platte River junction where a collage of signs appears through the tunnel of trees.

There are three canoe liveries at the crossroads: two on the near side of the river and a third across the bridge. On the far side of the river, just past the bridge, a road turns north beside a campground and winds its way through the woods down to the river mouth and the shores of Lake Michigan . . .

THE FIRST SEASON

In the beginning, all he heard about it was rumor. The government wanted to introduce big trout and salmon into Lake Michigan to feed on the alewives, the bait fish that had made their way through the locks into the Great Lakes and were now washing up dead on the beaches by the thousands. The trout and salmon would keep their numbers down and give sport fishermen something to be happy about, too. The government decided on coho salmon to do the job, and they wanted to start in the Platte River.

First it was the DNR trucks, passing on the road or stopping at the store for gas. And then when they built the hatchery on the upper river, and later the weir below Loon Lake, it was clear the salmon were on their way.

All that summer they worked to get ready. Logan built a cinderblock garage down at the river mouth and had a gas pump put in. He bought new skiffs and outboards and stocked the garage with fishing tackle. They sunk pilings in the river and built a makeshift dock. And when September came, the coho gathered in the bay just like they said. The coho came and so did the fishermen. They came by the thousands from all over the Midwest and Canada. They camped in the parks or stayed in hotels as far away as Cadillac.

Years later, Jack Young would remember the little things to make certain that it really happened that way. Waiting for a load of canoes, he'd look over to where the dock used to be before the Park took it out, and remember.

He was only fourteen then. But as more and more fishermen swarmed the main store at the bridge, Logan asked him if he could run things alone at the mouth. "Be smart," Logan told him. "Be smart and be tough."

He was always the first one there in the morning, with only the sound of the waves washing on the beach and the stars overhead. He'd top off the gas tanks and fill the oil jugs from the 55-gallon drum. Check each boat for oars, anchors, and cushions. Then to the garage to see that all was in order, ready to go: downriggers, cannonballs, poles, reels, leaders, and lures. By six o'clock there were cars and trucks and trailers lining both sides of the road for two miles, from the mouth of the river all the way up to the bridge.

It started before sunrise and didn't let up until the last boat was in at midnight. The early ones arrived in the dark, some of them still drunk from the night before. They came in boots and waders, vests and orange hunting caps, carrying thermoses and tackle boxes jammed with spoons and jigs meant for pond bass and bluegill. He'd show them the depth rigs, the dodgers and big plugs.

They'd pay their money and follow him down to the river where he showed them about the boat—the gas ball and air valve and choke, the throttle and gear levers and shear pins. Then he'd push them off and watch as they joined the throngs of other boats all jockeying and fighting to get out of the narrow mouth . . . down where the dredging crane stood like a dinosaur against the dawning sky.

And they'd keep coming and he'd outfit them, write up their licenses, pour gas, drain the oil jugs, joke right along with them, take their money and tips and brandy-laced coffee when they offered. He sold lures by the handful: J-plugs, spoons, tadpollies, flatfish, pink ladies, Manistee wobblers, dodgers in pink and white and chrome. Pounds of it crossing the counter at once and him banging the register, sending all those numbers spinning in the little glass window like a slot machine.

One night a boat stayed out late. When finally he heard it motoring up the river, the men were laughing and yelling. After he disconnected the gas line and secured the boat, they followed him to the shop.

"Hey, kid. You give refunds if we don't catch anything?"

"Don't blame it on the kid, Charlie," the biggest man said. "A bet is a bet and you're out fifty bucks."

Jack returned his license and locked the register.

The man named Charlie saw his .22 rifle in the corner and picked it up. "This yours, kid?" He raised the rifle and aimed for the mounted lake trout behind Jack. "I bet you're a pretty good shot."

The man named Charlie locked the bolt and held the gun across the arm of his hunting coat. "Do you ever bet, kid?" he said.

The others didn't move.

"I asked you if you ever bet."

"What do you want with the gun, Charlie?" said the big one.

Charlie turned and pointed it at the man's chest. The safety was free then.

"I'm going to win the kid some money," he said.

They followed him down to the retaining walls where the river narrowed up. One of the men held a flashlight over the water where they could see the dark backs of salmon swimming upriver. The man in the coat lowered the gun and shot into the river. With the box of cartridges, he reloaded and shot again.

The men took turns shooting with his gun. Some salmon floated downstream for the lake. Some thrashed in the shallow water along the far bank where the river turned cloudy with blood. In the yellow glare of the flashlight, Jack watched it all.

THE FIRST HE HEARD of it was over the short wave: a small craft warning for the eastern shore of Lake Michigan. Then later that next day when it looked worse, they called out the Coast Guard helicopters. They came in the day, broadcasting the warning over the lake.

Most fishermen got off but there were those who stayed out. Maybe they were like the local people said, flatlanders who'd never seen a lake storm before. Maybe too they saw the land just a mile away and figured they could always beach it. But these were skiffs and ten-foot dinghies with waterlines less than a foot deep.

The storm came at dusk and it hit like they said. The waves climbed to six feet, hammering the boats from every direction because that's the way lake storms go. Boats capsized. Fishermen were lost.

And the day after when the morning broke clear, he walked down to the mouth and saw all the debris washed up at the highline on the beach: coolers, cushions, oars, tackle, entire boats. All of it clear in the cold morning sunlight.

THINGS TO COME

In the years ahead, Jack learned how to fish the big lake with his brother Tom. The two brothers lived with their father in a cabin along Sleeping Bear cove, just up the coast from the river. Their cabin was built in the dunes behind the beach, protected from the wind and the big storms that came down from the north. Jack and his brother fished in a skiff they kept on the beach, trolling in the bay for brown trout in the spring, steelhead and lakers in the summer, and salmon in the fall. Then their father bought an old wooden fishing boat with a trailer that they could launch at the river mouth. In the early mornings before dawn, they hauled the boat down to the river so they could fish in the lake before work. Most mornings there was no one around and the river would be just like glass, with a thin line of fog along the horizon in the north. At first they fished together, Jack and his brother, but lately he went out alone.

It was no problem to go alone, he'd learned how to do it himself. After backing the trailer down the ramp, he unhitched the cable from the bow cleat and pushed the boat into the river. With the bowline, he pulled the boat upstream to the hard sand along the dirt lot where he beached it. Then he parked the car and trailer in the lot and loaded the rods and tackle into the boat. With the line coiled in his hand, he pushed off the sand and hopped in.

It was a quiet morning, and the boat floated down with the river current. A gray mist filled the woods behind the beach. Jack checked the controls behind the wheel, watching the river ahead. It was shallow near the launch, and he looked over the edge to see how deep it really was. He looked, but there was only his reflection in the wake of the boat. Drifting over the rocky shallows of the river, he saw his reflection on the surface in the empty color of sky.

The current carried his boat all the way outside the river mouth into Lake Michigan. Jack started the engine and headed for the drop-off in the bay. The air was cold and it was good to be out on the lake at dawn with the sky turning to blue, a far cry from this morning when he had first walked out. The sky then seemed on fire with stars, a cold white fire. Only the brightest stars remained now. There was Polaris in the north, shining true as ever.

When he was a mile offshore, he stopped the boat above the big shelf and prepared the gear. The poles and downriggers were set. He clipped on the cannon-balls and counted out seventy feet of line from the rod. Then he slid the line through the tension wheel and lowered both weight and line twenty feet down. He set the pin on the downrigger and reeled in the line until it was taut and the pole bent in a perfect arc. He did the same with the other rig, setting the line at fifteen feet. He set it all in place and returned to his seat behind the wheel.

He thought his brother was probably up by now back at the cabin. He would know by now that he went without him. He would wake up, see the white light of dawn, and know that he went without him again.

One of the poles went slack. Jack grabbed it out of the slot, jerked it once and reeled until the line tightened. But there wasn't much fight. Not like a lake trout that fought you from the bottom. He reeled the fish in easily and brought it alongside the boat. He could see right away that it was a jack. Leaning over the gunwale, he dislodged the hook and lowered the fish back into the water.

Before releasing it he held the young jack in his hands, turning it slowly in the lake. It was big enough to kill, but not really so old either. And that was all there was. He knew that was all. Some things you knew. And what you knew, you knew on account of what you didn't know. He could kill it. The salmon moved in his hands and swam away. He watched it swim down under the darkness of the lake.

Jack washed off the lure and threaded the line through the wheel on the downrigger cable, testing the tension. He swung the boom out and lowered the cannonball and line to the same depth on the counter.

Returning to the driver's seat, he checked the compass and steered for the big hole to the north.

A fleet of tall red clouds sailed over the tree line in the east. His brother would be ready for work by now, or close to it. He'd go in early today, Jack thought. Soon he'd ride the dirt bike down to the canoe livery on the corner and park it in the woods beyond the racks of canoes. One of the girls would be there to open the upstairs while he got things going by the river. He'd open the basement garage and drag a few canoes down to the docks like every morning. It was not a bad place to work and during the day there were a lot of people around. You didn't have to think too much about anything. In the early morning, there was no one around. His brother might sit alone then and wait for the sun, wait for it to rise over the trees and set the river flashing in white light.

A pole released.

Jack bolted up and reeled until he felt the weight. He reeled some more until the tension was too much and the fish made a run. When it stopped he reeled again, making sure to keep the rod up and the line taut with the fish.

He was cranking steadily when the pole jerked in his hands. The line screamed off the reel, angling away from the boat. The fish was in deep water a long way out. He tightened the drag but it was too much, the tension was too much. The line hissed out almost to the end. He had to reel. He was getting ready when the last of it came up loose around the reel, tangled in the spool.

The line lay slack across the water and he felt a little sick. It took a long while working it around, but he got it to where he felt the tension again and started to reel. He could tell by the weight that it was a good fish. He kept it even all the way in until the fish was close to the boat. He looked down once but saw only the line disappearing in the blue-green depths of the lake.

The fish moved to the back of the engine. He walked that way, keeping the tension on and the fish to the side of the boat. Nervous ripples spread from the line across the water surface. He reeled in what was given to him and looked again. Just below the surface, he saw the brown back of a trout weaving in the water.

Jack swooped the net under the fish and brought it into the boat. On the floor of the boat he freed the hook and held the live trout in his hands. The trout was golden brown, with spots the color of blood. He thought it was the most beautiful thing he'd ever seen. He liked the colors and the way the gills moved up and down with life. He thought he should keep it. He thought it was the most beautiful trout he'd ever caught. He put it in the box and closed the lid.

After washing off the blood, Jack let the line back out and raised the downrigger from the lake. He threaded the line through the wheel on the cannonball and lowered it to the same depth on the counter. He locked it all in place and returned to his seat behind the controls. His hands were still shaking from the fight. The trout made a sound in the box, and he switched on the depth finder.

He must be over the hole now because the bottom didn't register. It was the deepest part of the lake along the coast. He'd never been out this far before but it looked the same. The lake looked the same on the surface.

He was checking the drag in back when the sun broke free at the horizon. It came up red over the tree line. But the line of thunderheads sat right above, pressing down. The sun had barely risen before it slipped behind the bank of clouds and the morning went dark. When it was completely gone, the engine died.

Jack went to the front of the boat and checked the controls. It was quiet without the sound of the engine. He pulled the choke and turned the key. The starter turned over, but the engine wouldn't fire. He gave it more throttle and tried again. Still nothing. He turned the key a third time but the starter went into that long, drawn-out overload groan. He might have flooded it by now.

The trout made a sound in the box.

It was different without the engine on. He heard the waves now, lapping against the bottom of the boat. And the wind as it pushed him over the hole, the high sound of the wind against the taut fishing line.

Jack went to the back of the boat and looked inside the box. The colors of the trout were already fading. He closed the lid and looked across the lake to the north.

When it was time to try it again, he'd do it just like this morning. No choke, half throttle. He'd do it just like this morning.

CANOE IN THE LAKE

❖

On a hot day in June, Jack looked across the bay from the parking lot shore. All the canoes were on the trailer but the one out in the lake. Somehow it had escaped the river and now he could see it rising and falling in the waves, going out fast in the offshore wind. But there was the storm in the north. He could just strap everything in and head back to the store, tell Logan that one of his canoes was out in the lake with a storm moving in, and nobody would think twice.

Jack remembered the stories from the older boys, but he'd never seen it himself: a strong southwest wind, a canoe that wasn't pulled high enough on the beach. The canoe would drift out into the current and down the river into Lake Michigan. Then someone would have to drive a skiff out to tow it back. He remembered the older boys telling him about it, but now it was just him and his brother and Youngster who worked at the store. And there was the storm moving in from the north. He had all the canoes on but the one out in the lake. There was a skiff to pick up, too, but he could get that later with the boat trailer. He could just go back now and tell Logan.

Jack checked the skiff and made sure there was enough gas. He decided to see for himself what it was really like.

He pushed the boat into the river and started the outboard, steering for the middle of the current. The river ran smooth down to the mouth where the waves were breaking along the beach. He waited for his chance between waves. At just the right moment, he gunned the engine and the skiff launched over the surf into the lake.

Outside the point, he ran into the whitecaps coming up from the southwest. These were big sliding swells that had come all the way across the lake and they were easy to shoot. He only had to watch he didn't get caught in the bottom of a trough with a big wave breaking over him.

But there were different waves building off to the north. Out there, the water was mixing and churning. Wave spray whipped in the wind. The black edge of the squall crept overhead. He was looking for a way through it when the blast hit, a giant cold air blast. The bow blew off its heading and water sprayed over the gunwale. There would be rain and lightning before long, but it was the cold that stunned him. It shouldn't be so cold. He slowed the boat down and checked his position. He was a long way from shore. But if he went straight in and followed the sandbar back, he would surely be safe.

Jack steered the bow into the crosswind and started for the canoe. It made little difference to steer through the waves since they came fast now and from all sides. When the rain started it made a thousand rings on the water. The rain fell harder until it seemed to roar and he saw it streaking over the lake.

When he got to the canoe he set the motor in neutral and scrambled to the front of the boat. All he had was the anchor line to lash the canoe. He placed the anchor in the bow and towed it until the weight dragged the canoe over. It would sink before he ever got it in. He tried the knot, but it was cold and hard as iron. Lightning flashed everywhere. He didn't really care about the canoe anyway.

There looked to be a sharp enough edge in the oarlock. He moved to the middle seat and threaded the rope through the lock. He grabbed it underneath and worked it hard against the edge, pulling the line back and forth through the oarlock, but it was no good. The metal edge was too dull to cut the rope.

The stern drifted around to the north, into the waves. He was working the line when a rogue wave crested over the transom and threw the boat into a slide. Jack fell to the bottom of the boat, looking up in the rain. A jagged white streak splintered the sky and everything stopped for a moment, frozen in the lightning.

Jack swung the boat around and reached for the sunken canoe. Against the drag of all the water, against the driving rain and lightning, he raised the canoe from the lake. In a last awful heave he pulled it from the water and loaded it in the skiff.

He sat down in the boat and looked across the water. The rain fell in long steady sheets over the lake. He had the canoe in the boat now and all that was left to do was to drive back to the river. He'd gotten the canoe and all that he had to do was to drive back. Jack listened to the rain falling on the lake. It seemed to be letting up. The storm was already moving off. He set the boat in gear and started for shore.

The squall blew off the lake and moved across the land. When the sun broke free, he could see it over the tree line in the south. The back side of it was lit up and glorious to look at.

But he kept watch of the storm. The heart of it was dark and defiant and it trembled with lightning. He watched the storm and the torrents of black rain falling over the land.

THE WILD UPRIVER

J ack looked up from the beach to see the killdeer div-
ing through the sun. The bird swept past in a trail
of sharp, urgent cries that died out in the distance. He
watched it for as long as he could—flying along the
shore toward the river point, rising in the sky somewhere above the steep bluff outside the mouth. Everything was ready now. He placed his gun and a
shovel in the bottom of the skiff, pushed the boat from
shore, and started the outboard.

It was only a mile from their cabin on Lake Michigan to the mouth of the river. He drove the skiff at
full throttle, following the sandbar along the beach.

From the lake he could see the broad sweep of dune country along the coast, the plains of grass and big bowls of sand, the edge of the woods along the back ridge. Patches of sand cherry and wild grape grew in the dunes. Behind him, the coastline curved northward to Empire bluff and Sleeping Bear dune across the bay. Off the point of Sleeping Bear, he could see the back side of South Manitou Island shining in the afternoon sun.

The lake was flat, and the skiff ran smooth over the water. Outside the mouth a flock of gulls and terns drifted on the water. If he steered right for them they would all fly off together. He always liked riding into the heart of a big flock and seeing the birds rise everywhere around him. He liked how they waited until the last moment before picking up to fly.

Once, one of the terns didn't fly off. He had driven through the flock as always only one of the birds didn't rise up. He circled back in his boat and still the tern stayed in the water, dragging one of its wings in the lake. He lifted the bird out of the lake and folded the wing under his hands, holding it in his lap all the way back to the cabin. The tern had a wild look in its eyes, and once it reared back and bit him in the hand.

He kept the bird close to the cabin, out of the wind. He gave it water and bait fish out of the lake. On the third day he put it on the beach and watched from a distance. The tern flew twenty feet and dropped into the lake. Then he stretched his wings and was gone for good.

The terns outside the mouth looked colorless against the lake, like animal bones in moonlight. He steered around them and headed for the river.

The lake was high that year. If he could find the flat water right away and keep to the edge of the rock pile, he could make it into the river without letting up on the throttle. He found the channel by the ripple in the current and ran the sandbar full speed into the river.

Staying to the right of the channel, he steered around a second line of rocks at the boat ramp and headed for the narrow strait between the two retaining walls. At normal levels the river flowed through the strait, but now there was water behind the walls and halfway up the dirt parking lot. The river was high, too.

The banks of the lower river were crowded with cottages built by summer people from downstate. They were quaint little homes trimmed in yellow and orange, but they were a lie and that was the worst thing of all. He hated that worst of all. Most of the cottages were flooded out, the wells ruined. Jack steered perfect curves through the bends, satisfied with the way his wake lapped up against the prefab siding. If he wanted to, he could run the entire five miles of river at full throttle all the way to the pine arbor.

Jack slowed the skiff after running the weir gate. From here to the lake there was nothing but willow and wild rose riverside, where snappers sunned themselves on big snags and muskrat patrolled the shallows, and where in November a single salmon egg put down just right could get you a 10-pound rainbow. He slowed the boat all the way down for the watersnake winding through the river.

When he first had seen the fawn, it came running through the meadow like it was the tall bay grass itself taken to flight. And when it came running out beside the doe and it must have seen the truck because they began to turn and he saw them through the passenger window running alongside the truck, and when it looked like they were going to be in the clear and the fawn dropped like a stone, its legs caught under the front wheel, he thought it would still get up and run back to the woods. And after he circled back in the truck and saw the fawn bleating on the road, three of its legs hanging useless there and the doe watching from the edge of the woods, he was sure there was something he could do.

Jack moved the skiff slowly through the outlet, looking for the loon nest in the hummocks along the leeward shore. The high water had killed the trees in back of the river. They loomed in the sky, bare and weather gray. In the shore grass, he saw the loon and the ring on its neck like some necklace.

He didn't tell anyone about it, about how he was finally able to carry the fawn upriver to the hidden pine arbor, how it wanted nothing at first but just to get away.

It didn't take long to cross the inland lake once he opened the throttle again and the skiff pounded against the chop. A blue heron flew along the shore, its big wings pressing and releasing in that gangly loping motion in front of the trees. There was not much beach around the lake, and even the spit of sand at the inlet was flooded over. Jack swung the skiff wide around the point and picked up the channel between the sandbars. From here to the pine arbor, it was only another two bends to go.

He has found it one day looking for a place to hide. He was in trouble and needed a place to go. He'd been to the old abandoned dock on the wild stretch below the weir. It was a place where he could be alone in the old forest, where he could crawl out on the dock and if he was good enough surprise a salmon with his spear. Like the old Indians, he could hunt them. It took a long time to get it right and even then he only killed one. He speared a king and there was nothing like it, fighting a king to the end with all the water splashing in the sunlight back there in the old woods. When the DNR boat came speeding around the bend, he walked into the trees and started upriver. He went deep into the woods, as far as he could go, and worked his way up. He could have gone home or made it to the livery, but it wasn't like that. He would find the deepest woods and stay there for as long as it took. He went past the weir and further up, above the lake.

Jack tied the skiff to a tree and walked through the brambles along the river. Outside the pine trees he slid a bullet in with his free hand and thought about the fawn inside.

In the pine arbor, he liked the way the sun streamed down to the pools of light on the needle floor.

He had killed many times before this. He only had to walk in, be done with it, and never think about it again.

He liked the deep green water by the bank, the dreamy way the sunlight splintered down to the rocks on the bottom. It was a good place to go where nothing could touch him.

It was the civil thing to do, the only thing.

When it was done he buried the fawn under the pine trees. It was the only thing to do. He buried it deep and covered the hole with rocks, so wild dogs wouldn't dig it up too soon.

THIS IS THE DEAL

❖

Jack ran the river with all seven-and-a-half horses wide open, in the skiff they called the Shark for the black maw and menacing teeth painted on the bow—dipping past the boat ramp and lily shallows, carving up the big bends of the lower river and the oxbow turn where he stole his first kiss at the sand hill. Now past the swimming hole and the docks of the summer cabins, and further up, through the open weir gate where in the fall the salmon don't have it so lucky. Slowing down at the outlet where the loons and heron nest, then across the choppy lake where sand shot jarred loose from the skiff's ribs and thwarts stung his face. Back into the river again, through the shallow rock garden gleaming white and copper in quicksilver sunlight—at the bend where the old Indian lived in his hideaway cabin and where once he sheared a pin and lost his prop.

This time he ran the rock garden clean. Seven miles of river and not once backing down to the snag-studded river bends, with nothing to stop him from here on out but the old lady on her dock.

Around the turn at cedar bend, and there she was. He waited until she placed her hands on the arms of her chair before slowing down. Too many times she had run out to the end of her dock, screaming and shaking her fist, with that yellow "Slow Down!" sign on the tree behind her, while the wake from his boat rolled up on the banks of the river.

The engine coughed and sputtered with the slow speed. He waved. She nodded once.

Coming around the last bend, Jack saw that *Waterside* had a sprinkler going in their yard. *Waterside* was the newest of the three canoe liveries on the corner, run by a couple who wintered in Florida. He wore shiny white shoes. She had dirt hauled in and planted lawn grass that looked like the artificial turf they laid out in front of the hardware store in town. She planted flowers too, flowers Jack had never seen before. Tulips, daffodils, and ugly orange lilies.

At full throttle he cut a sharp turn in front of the canoes drifting between the docks. The heavy wake set the canoes banging against each other as two boats inched their way into the current. The lady proprietor stormed across her lawn, yelling at him, "Slow . . . reporting you . . . !"

Then he was gone, drawn through the concrete girders of the bridge. The skiff emerged in the sun on the other side where Youngster was waiting in his boat with another boy, waving upriver.

"Keep going!" he cried. "We'll meet you at Cut-throat Cove!"

Jack steered the Shark through the last two bends to Big Platte Lake. He followed the channel out, then turned hard along the north shore. This was the last wild stretch left on the lake. He drove all the way to the back of the cove and pulled the Shark up on the beach.

Youngster came in right behind him. The other boy hopped out and watched as Youngster pulled the boat up by himself. Youngster had taken to growing his hair long. It was past his shoulders now and white as snow. The other boy wore a muscle shirt and a buck knife on his belt.

"This is Sandy," said Youngster. "Maybe you've seen him in Frankfort. He's first mate on the *Fair Wind*."

Jack noticed the small scar on his temple. "That's what's-his-name's boat, isn't it?"

"Kirk Laidlaw," said Sandy.

Jack knew who it was, all right. When he was smaller Jack had taken the Van Duzee sisters to the swimming hole on the river. Kirk Laidlaw and two of his Frankfort friends hassled them so bad that they had to leave.

"Catching anything these days?" asked Jack.

"Oh yeah," said the first mate. "We're very good. Kirk's father's going to buy us a new outfit this fall. We're going to charter winters in Florida."

"That so?"

"Yeah," he said. "Fish for tarpon and bonito."

A blue jay squawked sharply in the trees behind the beach.

"Did you bring any bonito with you today?"

"Got it right here," said Sandy.

The first mate went back to the skiff and returned with a paper bag. He took out a half dozen plastic wraps and spread them on the sand.

"That's good stuff there," he said. "Best in the county."

Jack took up one of the nickel bags and fingered the leafy weed through the plastic. He'd never seen it before. "Looks kind of skimpy for a nickel."

The boy reached into the bag and culled another handful of wraps.

"Here's a couple more," he said. "Take your pick."

"I don't know," said Jack, shaking his head.

"It's really good stuff," said the first mate. "It's like *wow*, you know?"

Jack held the wraps in his hand. "These are five, right?"

"Seven."

"*Seven?*" blurted Jack. "I thought these were nickels."

"They are."

"So why is it you're selling me a nickel for seven?"

"Unflation," quipped the proud first mate. "It's good stuff, man. I'm telling you. It makes me feel good to turn people on to it. It's my scene."

Youngster just shrugged. He'd told Jack at work that he knew where to get some. Now he slipped his hands in his pockets and toed a stick in the sand.

"I don't have seven," said Jack. "I only brought five."

"Can't do it," said the first mate.

"Then I'll see you later," said Jack.

When he was well offshore and speeding across the lake, Jack pulled the stolen wrap from his pocket.

It gleamed in his hand like a shiny silver dollar. He looked back and saw the first mate reaching through his bag in the bow of Youngster's boat.

On the way down the river, his wake rolled up on the banks and sent everything bobbing in the tumult. The floating docks ground against their moorings. The white buoys swung and twisted like craning heads. Youngster's skiff followed right behind. The first mate looked stern and grim, his arms splayed to the gunwales like guide wires.

Coming out the other side of the bridge, Jack waved to the deputy standing next to the lady proprietor who wintered in Florida. Then it was Youngster's turn. At full bore he burst through the dark underpass into the sunshine where the lady was now yelling at the deputy. Loose canoes spilled from their slips and littered the river. Before disappearing around the bend, Jack looked back and saw the police skiff picking its way through the shiny aluminum canoes.

He didn't have the horsepower to outrace either Youngster or the deputy. His only chance was the shallow strait to Mud Lake. He'd been through there once but only in a canoe. There was nothing in there but dead water and mud.

Up ahead he saw the narrow break in the reeds. At full throttle he swung a wide turn in the river and pointed the bow for the passage. The skiff charged up the narrow strait and for a minute it seemed just like running a four-wheel down a flooded-out fire road. The skiff was well off the river when he saw the break in the trees over Mud Lake. There would be plenty of places around the lake to hide the boat. There was even that opening on the back corner where he could get a trailer down to the water. Rounding the last bend, it looked like he would make it. The break in the woods grew wider and brighter and he hardly noticed when the hull started its slow, one-way slide onto mud. The Shark glided to a stop and he was dead in the water, not a stone's throw from Mud Lake.

Jack turned off the engine.

The steady groan of Youngster's skiff swelled in the trees behind him. The prow and the first mate came knifing into view when Youngster's bigger, heavier skiff slid up on the mud twenty feet behind. Then the deputy rode his double-hull up beside Youngster.

"I KNOW SHE'S A witch," said the half blood deputy to his cousin in the middle boat. "But there's a speed limit on the river."

They were close enough that they all just talked from their boats.

"Where's your hydroplane, anyhow?" he asked.

"Up at the store," said Youngster. "I have to straighten out the steering cable yet."

The water still bubbled and frothed from all the racing, settling out black and muddy around the boats.

"It leaks too," said Jack.

The tamarack fronds hung in the air. Everything was still in the heavy bog air.

"When are you going to have it ready?" asked the deputy. "I want to run mine once before the Elberta race."

"It'll be ready," Youngster replied.

"You know, you would never won last year if you hadn'ta cheated and I know you did, so don't deny it. What'd you do anyway, put in a bigger carb? Maybe you fiddled with the governor."

"I ain't telling," said Youngster.

The deputy rested against his outboard in the far boat. "I just picked up a bigger prop," he said. "See if that don't make a difference."

In the woods around the lake a mourning dove cried, *Nooo nooo nooo!*

"The old Indian downriver gave it to me."

"I bet it's black," said Jack.

"Used to be," he said. "It's all nicked up and wore smooth by now. Still good, though."

That's all the deputy was going to say about it.

The four of them just sat there, silent and still in the grounded boats. It seemed the deputy made absolutely certain there was nothing more to talk about.

"Okay son," he said. "Give me that bag you have there."

The first mate hesitated, then threw the bag into the police boat. The deputy pulled out the plastic wraps and held them in his hand.

"Where you from?" he asked.

"Town," said the first mate.

The deputy placed the wraps back in the bag and rolled the whole thing up.

"You know," he said, as the light of the sky flashed off his badge. "You know, just last summer a deer tried walking through all this mess and got stuck. Got stuck and sunk all the way up to its withers."

The deputy placed the bag under his seat and stared across the lake, like he was looking for something in all the bog and mud.

"Finally the flies just et him alive," he said. "Looked like they went after his eyes first. They was all sunk in and hollow."

THE THREE BOYS PUSHED the dual-hull with the deputy still sitting at the helm. The mud was deep and sucked at their feet. As they were pushing, Jack and Youngster saw a loose *Waterside* canoe floating down the river. When the deputy drove his skiff upriver out of sight, the first mate drew his knife.

"Just what do you think you're doing?" he said to Jack.

The first mate fidgeted and swung the knife to the other hand.

"You stole a bag," he said.

"So what?" said Jack.

"So, I want it back."

Nooo nooo, cried the dove.

"Give it to me," said the first mate.

"It's not *fair*, is it?" said Jack.

"Give it to me. You stole it."

They were all three sinking deeper in the mud. Jack waited, not caring how the first mate wanted to get out of this.

Finally, Youngster leaned over and tried raising one of his legs. It made a sucking noise in the mud. "Come on, Sandy," he said. "Let's just hoot some of that stuff and call it even."

"But he stole it."

"Shut up," said Jack.

The first mate was silent and a little glum as they smoked in the mud. This was the first time for Youngster and Jack. It did nothing at all for them, and they thought very little of it in the end.

NORTHERN LIGHTS

❖

"We could be riding there on a cloud."
Floating through the fog, they were all just voices in the dark.

"Flying clouds," she said. "Into the light, mysterious light."

"The *big* light," said Tom.

They could see the lights in the north, flashing and streaking across the sky.

"I can't see," said Youngster, sitting up in his seat. "The dark . . . ."

Jack paddled to keep them straight. The river was warm and still as glass, reflecting the stars in the breaks of fog.

In the far canoe, Logan watched the lights and said nothing.

"Oh, I see 'em now," barked Youngster, touching off a round of soft laughter. Youngster had the genuine northern voice, smoke-husky and loud. "I see the light," he said.

Laura leaned back and looked straight into the cold light of the stars. She had only started working in July, but Jack knew about her before then. She was a summer girl from downstate. She lived in a cottage upriver and sometimes she rode her boat down to the store. He finally figured out something to say to her, but he didn't figure on all the rest. In the night that looked faintly blue, there were thousands of stars blinking separately in space.

"It's the end," his brother said, "that one-way ride into the light, the end."

Jack wished he would stop. There was no use talking about it. There was no use talking about a lot of things.

"What do you think, Jack?" he said, getting himself another beer. "You're awful quiet tonight."

Logan struck a match in the far canoe. The flame burst round and full, then died in a hiss on the river.

"Wouldn't it be nice," she said, in a voice sweet as a meadowlark. "Wouldn't it be nice to fly?"

It was all over, summer was gone. It was the end of another season. No more car shuttles down to the mouth, no more hauling canoes back to the store. It was the time of year when the nights grew cold, when fog crept across the river into the woods. They were all together for the annual midnight canoe trip down the river. They were together for the last time of summer, floating along in the dark with the northern lights burning up the sky, streaking across the night to light up the sky.

"Look, there's the sand hill," said Youngster. "Remember, we stay dry this summer."

"That's right," said Tom, putting down his beer. "Everybody stays dry."

They did it the same way every year.

"Youngster, why don't you give Logan a hand getting in?" said Jack.

Youngster hopped into the waist-high water and waded toward the far canoe.

"That's okay," said the young storeowner. "I can see my way clear."

"No," said Jack, jumping in. "It has to be this way."

He waded around the back as Youngster approached from the front. The warm water made the air feel even colder. They would get Logan first, then Laura and Tom.

"It really is most kind," Logan said. "But we can see ourselves in."

"I insist," said Jack.

"You're too kind."

But before they could dump him, Logan stood up in the canoe and dove into the dark river. That was the way with him. He always went one further. Jack had come to know this about his friend and never passed up the chance to see him do it again, to see how far he would go. They all wanted to see just how far he'd go, but especially Jack.

Tom rolled his canoe alone while Jack gently tipped Laura. Paddles and cushions bobbed in the river current. All of it floated toward the oxbow bend where the sand hill came down to the river. In the reflection of stars shining on the water, Jack found the sealed tin holding the matches.

WHILE THE OTHERS WAITED IN the river, he and Logan built a fire on top of the hill. Jack knew right where to find the dry dune grass and deadfall. He came here often to swim and hike in the dunes.

"Be sure to stop by the store tomorrow," Logan said. "I left a little something for you."

The fire caught fast as a whirl of sparks lifted off the grass and spiraled for the stars.

"A bonus," he said. "We got a lot done this year. It was a good year."

It might have been the play of firelight but it seemed something flashed in his eyes, the way ash goes dark when the wind blows. Logan had this way of changing suddenly to deadly serious. Sometimes it happened so fast Jack couldn't tell one from the other. Roni said it was from the six months he spent in a Vietnam hospital and not to worry about it. But it never escaped Jack. He saw it in terms of good and bad, that for every good thing there's a bad one, and as far as you go in one direction you can be sure to go in the other.

"I mean it, Jack. It means a lot . . ."

"Logan, you don't have to."

". . . to us, with the new baby on the way now. Thanks for what you've done."

"Logan . . . ."

But Jack couldn't say it. He never could. He was never good at that sort of thing, and now whatever it was that he didn't know to say got stuck in his throat.

It was the kind of thing he thought was best to forget anyway.

But it wasn't that way with Logan, and he knew it. They came in the spring, Roni and Logan, two years earlier. He was just a kid then but he told Logan what he knew about running canoes, about the shuttles and repairs. He told him about the fishing skiffs, the outboards and maintenance, the bait shop, and all that went with the marina—the parts and tools, the lower-unit grease, the plugs and hoses and points. He told him about the salesmen and drunks and highwaymen, careful to look at him when he said it. Logan listened but Jack couldn't help feeling that he knew about it already, knew about it in fact long ago. Maybe not the particulars of running a canoe business, but everything else.

He remembered the rainy day Logan sent him to Crystal Lake to pick up a boat. The road was flooded out with rainwater and every time he plowed the truck through one of those long puddles a little more moisture worked its way under the distributor cap, so when it came time to haul out the boat he cranked the truck over and over again, swearing he'd get it back to the store without Logan or anyone else to help him. And then a week later when the new starter was delivered, he was down by the river getting everything ready for the midday rush. Logan called him up and together they put the starter in. At the busiest time of day, while Tom and Youngster ran ragged around the yard with canoes, Logan and he tore into the engine in the shade of the truck—hands greasy and sand working its way under his shirt and all he could think was why, if for no other reason, why was Logan doing this for him?

And now all he could do was plow some sand with his foot and say he was going for more wood.

There would be another time. There was always another time. Logan didn't need to hear it from him anyway. Hell, he had a Purple Heart.

"That fire hot enough?"

Youngster walked up and dragged a pine limb over the flames.

"There," he said. "See how that does."

The flames cracked and hissed with the new log.

"And who's got you all fired up tonight?"

As the flames reached higher, the others came up and sat close around the fire.

"How many beers have you had, anyway?" Jack continued.

"I'm allowed," said Youngster, the ire rising in his pale blue eyes.

"I think he had two," Tom said.

"I can!"

The firelight made it hard to see and Jack moved away until he saw the stars and dunes again and the darkness over the bay. From down on the beach, he heard the quiet sigh of the surf.

"Salmon ought to be here by now," said Tom.

"Another week or two," Youngster replied. "And then they'll be ready."

The waves were down tonight, the lake was calm.

"They gather together, don't they?" asked Laura. "For the day when they all run together?"

On the other side of the hill, the river fog snaked through the woods into the distance.

"What makes them do that?" she asked. "Gather all together like that then one day just take off upriver?"

"They just know is all," said Youngster. "What makes anything do what it does?"

"But what makes them always come back to the same place, to die?"

"They just *know*," he said again. "What makes you stare into the stars? What makes Logan do all his crazy things? What makes Jack think he's always got to fight everything clear through to the other side, just to see what's there?"

An ember popped in the fire, scattering sparks around their feet.

"Same thing that makes you a cuss," Jack said.

"See what I mean?"

Logan laughed, Laura came closer, and it was all right like this. The fire was hot with a nice bed of coals and a good light. They were all together. They were all together and as long as they were there, it was all right.

THE SAND ON THE TRAIL felt cool between his toes. There was nothing on this side of the river but the wild dune country rolling down to the lake—the hills and bowls patchworked with juniper, dune grass, and sand cherry. This was the country Jack loved more than all the rest, more than the deep woods and river though he loved those too. There was something about standing high atop a dune and seeing all that blue water out there, the islands and two bluffs across the bay. Sometimes at night the lake looked like a black space that went on forever. It made him think of all the shipwrecks and lost souls he knew to be at the bottom, but even that seemed as it should be now. He could see another bonfire flickering up the coast. There might be a half dozen bonfires on a night like this, each rising out of darkness to burn and fall again to the night. He wanted them to see his fire. He wanted them all to see his fire like he now saw theirs.

He saw Laura coming down the trail, walking through the dunes in the blue light of darkness.

"I was looking for you," she said.

Her hair was blond like many summer girls. As she looked up, a lock of it blew across her face and it seemed then that there was all the time in the world.

"Aren't they wonderful?"

Jack turned and looked again at the strange lights in the north.

"You're leaving soon," he said.

"Tomorrow," said Laura. "Will you come see me?"

"Sure," he said.

"Before it snows?"

"Sure."

"Jack, what's wrong?"

"Nothing."

"Why don't you tell me?"

"There's nothing to tell."

"Then why are you like this?"

A tern cried over the lake.

"Stay with me tonight," she said. "Out here on the dunes."

As she came closer he heard the lone tern again in the darkness over the lake.

"You and me together, Jack," she said. "One last time."

Up the coast, the bonfires flickered one by one. There was a fire at the end of the lake road and he wondered who was there. Maybe some of his friends from Honor, drinking and telling stories. Maybe someone like Laura who would give him that feeling the first time he saw her. Maybe she would feel it too, and they could walk down the beach and talk and see how it all matched up.

IN THE TREES
FURTHEST BACK

❖

By September of that year, the woods had already
begun to change color. First it was the trees along
the roads, their leaves suddenly gone bright yellow.
Sumac turned deep red in the meadows, and golden-
rod bloomed in the dunes. On warm Indian summer
days, a smoky haze filled the air over the lake where
Canada geese flew down from the north. Sometimes,
while working at the store, Jack would stop what he
was doing to watch and listen as the big birds flew
past.

By the middle of October, the woods were ablaze
with the reds of maple and oak, the yellows of beech,

the greens of hemlock and fir. Soon, it was cold enough each morning to see a glaze in the river shallows. Jack and his brother worked for Logan through salmon season, but after that there was nothing much to do. The colors of autumn faded to the clouds and cold of November, as north winds blew the first storms in. By the end of that month, the woods were bare and wet from an early winter's snowfall.

Watching the trees go by from his seat in the pickup truck, Jack looked first at the closer ones moving so fast he had to strain to make them out separately. He looked further in at the dark limbs of bigger trees following a slower pace. Then deep in the woods where the shadows were darkest, he saw the trunk of an old oak that seemed to be moving at the same speed as the pickup. He watched it for as long as he could until it too faded back to nothing.

The driver of the truck said he could take him all the way to town if he wanted. He didn't talk much, which suited Jack all right. A shiny new carburetor rested on the seat between them. The driver's hands were black with engine grease and when he reached down to steady it, the metal carb seemed even brighter. Jack was happy just to ride along to the hum of the engine, certain that the mechanic had lived his whole life in town.

The man slowed down for the flashing light at the junction. On one corner, an old boarded-up store leaned against a trailer-home buried in dead grass. Across from that was a tumbledown cabin that might have once been the saloon. The pickup came to a stop, and Jack got out at the light.

When the truck drove away, he heard it for a long time afterward going down the road for a vanishing point way off in the blue distance. All four roads here stretched flat and straight for as far as he could see. They cut straight and even into a vast expanse of dark Michigan woods. He could go any direction, it didn't matter. When the sound of the truck wheels faded, he heard the high wail of a faraway diesel.

He was alone at a crossroads he'd never seen before. He wasn't sure where he was, but he had come this way and it looked like a good place to get out. There was something peaceful about it, about all the space. He liked the feel of the road under his boots and the wind in his hair—the way the land was brown and dead, surrendered to winter. It was a good place to be alone.

After awhile, he heard a car coming down the road through the long gauntlet of trees. It was an old sixties sedan with out-of-state plates and he crossed over to wait for it. As the car geared down for the junction, he heard the wind in the hollow insides of the cabin. The car slowed all the way down and stopped beside him.

"Hi," said a woman through the open window. She had an easy smile and could have been his same age.

Jack looked up at the long blue arc of highway reaching to the horizon, listening to the wind as it blew through the timbers of the cabin.

He opened the door and got in.

"Kind of a bad day to be traveling around," she said, running the car through the gears.

"You get used to it, I guess," he said.

"But it's so dreary."

He noticed all the traveling gear in the back. There were duffel bags and boxes packed behind the seats.

"And dark," she said. "It's been cold and dark like this for so long I can hardly remember the sun. And the wind. It seems like it's been blowing forever. Snow would be better. At least with snow everything is covered and it doesn't all seem so bleak, so dark."

He could feel her watching him.

"But you don't seem to mind," she said.

"It's the storm season now," said Jack. "It's not for everybody, but I like it all right."

"Is that why northerners are so friendly?"

He looked down at the mud on his boots, remembering the safety of the junction. He was alone there. Alone with nothing around but the space and high diesel wail.

"Where are you headed?" she asked.

"How far are you going?"

"I'm going to Canada," she said. "For the winter."

"That's quite a ways."

She pulled some of her long brown hair behind her ear and looked at him.

"I have a brother there," she said. "I haven't seen him since I was a little girl, since the war. I was never allowed to see him. He was a C.O."

Jack looked out at the trees. The closer ones rushed past in a blur.

"You don't talk very much," she said.

The road was wet from the earlier snow and now the tires hissed over the pavement.

"Do you think he was right?" he asked.

"He's a C.O.," she said. "I don't see a right and wrong."

Again, he looked out the window.

"Do you?"

"No," said Jack. "I guess not."

The sky was heavy with snow. Wet snow and rain.

"What do you say we smoke?" she grinned. "The peace pipe."

"Good," he said in a voice that sounded awkward to him, a voice too willing. But the moment passed and he told himself to pay attention now, because every second counted with her and already she was reaching into her pocket while steering with the hand that held the pipe.

"Here," he said, and brought out a lighter. He got it going and handed it back, watching as she took the pipe. Her hair fell forward again and he looked at her bracelets and rings. She had a ring for every finger, rings of silver, turquoise and coral, but the one he noticed was the silver filigree on her first finger. It was tarnished on the edges and big enough to cover half her finger. He looked closely and saw a girl in a tunic, with long hair, surrounded by plants and flowers. She handed him the pipe and he looked closer still. It looked like a goddess of some kind.

He liked this girl, and he was miserable. He remembered the nameless junction and the way the dead grass had reclaimed the shacks, the sheer aloneness of it all. But before he was even finished with the thought he knew that it was hollow, not true. He tried looking out at the white lines, but he couldn't seem to see beyond the dirty windshield.

She handed him the pipe again. The smoke curled in front of him and he watched it twist and turn, always rising.

"You didn't say where you were going."

"I'm not going anywhere," he said. "I'm just going."

"You're just out here hitchhiking around, going nowhere?"

"That's right," he said and looked away. "I have my reasons."

"I believe you," she said.

"Nobody has to understand."

"It's okay," she said. "Really."

He tried looking into the deepest woods, for the big oak trees hiding out. Looking out.

The girl moved her hand and the silver bracelets jangled on her wrist. It sounded magical with all the drab countryside rolling by outside.

Jack sighed and turned away from the woods. "That's not what I meant to say either," he said.

"So, why *are* you out here?" she asked.

She looked at him, and for the first time he saw her eyes. They were light and clear like the pieces of green glass that wash up on the beach. But there was something distant there too, like a part of her was gone away.

The road entered the woods again. There was more traffic now and he knew where he was.

"There's a turnoff up ahead," he said. "It goes down to a bluff above the beach. It's a good place to watch the storm come in."

He knew most of the county backroads and traveled on them when he could, especially the ones that went deep into the woods. Back there he didn't feel strange like he did in the open. It was like a lot of things. Sometimes he felt locked into sights he didn't understand, sights that wanted something from him. Back in the woods he didn't feel all the eyes. He was traveling backroads before he even knew the difference.

She drove to the end of the road and parked where they could see the storm over the lake. He rolled his window down to hear the wind and the sound of the waves on the beach. From high atop the bluff, the sky looked dark and close enough to almost touch. The whitecaps rolled in from the north, and for as far as he could see there was only the storm.

"I guess I wanted to be alone," he said. "But it's good to see someone like you."

There was something strange in the way she looked at him now. It seemed she looked through him, to something beyond him.

She turned away and her hair fell forward, hiding her eyes. She twisted the silver ring around her finger, and he looked again at her long flowing hair.

She could have been his sister.

"I was a dancer once," she said. "I was good, too. They came from a long way to see me and once I got up to dance they never looked away. I could feel their eyes on me because it would get very quiet, and when I did look at them I could tell. It wasn't that way with the other girls. I would dance slowly because I could feel everything better that way, everything that was my life. And it was like a dream for me too, I guess, a real long sad dream. A dream of another time and other dreams all gone now, but still good—even now. Dreams of a family and a house with a big bell I could ring and listen for as the sound carried over the hills."

She stopped for a moment and looked into the storm.

"It was different after that. I moved around a lot. If things went bad, I moved. If they were good, I ended up tearing it all down. Do you know what I mean? I saw through it all. The lies, I mean. There's a lie with everything, you know. Even this story I'm telling you now."

She smiled with the storm outside, almost like a girl.

"Then it was too late for me," she said. "I'd shot everything clear through so as to never be the same. I've done some things, you know. I think you know."

She tugged at the frayed end of her shirt as the wind came through the open window. It was starting to snow again.

"Out here there's nothing, and that's what it all comes down to. There's no one to say one way or the other for you. Mostly, there's no one at all."

On the dark afternoon her eyes looked bright and clear and he thought he knew about her. With the wind roaring through the open windows, he thought he knew about her but it didn't matter. Nothing mattered now about her, about him.

She drove back up the two-track, out to the highway. When they were close to town he told her to stop and he would get out.

"Tell me this," she said, slowing all the way down at the side of the road. "What could you believe in?"

They were close to town in a howling wind. He wanted to tell her about the big trees deep in the woods that stayed the same no matter what. Tell her there were times when he was sure in his mind that he was perfect. Tell her sometimes even that was not enough.

Before he went, he looked at her through the open window. She was as beautiful as he had thought all along, in the way a woman can be.

"Maybe in the spring," he started. "If you come back this way. I live west of here by the river."

He was about to go, but he looked again into the green eyes that just then seemed strangely familiar. "My name is Jack," he said. "Jack Young."

SNOWED IN

❖

In the afternoon, he walked down the lane to see if they could get out. The storm had started the day before and by nightfall it was a blizzard. Now, it was all he could do to find the road in the blowing snow. When he reached the bend and saw that the drift was too high, he went further to where the lane entered the woods. He walked in until it was quiet and the snow fell softly between the trees. It could be days before they got out. They'd have to wait for the front-end loader, and there was no telling how long that would be.

The lane followed a white gap through the bare woods, narrowing out in the distance. After a while he heard the sound of falling snow on the ground and the wind in the trees. He watched the wind high in the tops of the trees, moving off to the south. He would stay in the woods until the cold drove him back, and it might seem he was gone too long.

When the big storms came down from the north, there was nothing much to do. The wind blew straight off the lake, driving the snow into deep drifts across the dunes. Their cabin was built behind the first beach dune and most times they could get out. But when the big northers blew, they could be snowed in for days. They just had to wait it out. Keep the fire burning and wait it out.

When he returned to the cabin, his father showed him the deer.

Jack focused on the patch of brown in the driving snow offshore. It was a buck, and he stood on one of the ice floes that had blown in with the wind. In a quick powerful move, the deer leapt to another piece of ice.

"He's making his way over here," his father said, stoking the fire. "All the way across the bay. That must be five miles."

Jack lowered the binoculars as sparks snapped in the fire. He looked again and saw the buck leap in the storm. This time the deer slipped off the ice and fell into the lake up to his haunches. Then he lost him in the blowing snow.

"The drift at the corner is too high for the jeep," he said.

His father stood up and looked at him. He was a big man, wide in the chest. The silver curls around his head were close and furious. "Phones are out, too," he said. "I'll walk down for supplies before dark."

"We're all set for tonight," said Jack. "I made sure we have enough for tonight."

"I'll go," said his father, pointing to the bar. "Get yourself a drink."

Jack poured the whiskey carefully over the ice and sat down by the fire. From where he sat, he could see the white spread of the storm over the bay.

"Down at the store, they say it was a bad year for the salmon," his father said. "But you got a few. Then again, you were out there for three weeks solid."

Outside, the waves raged against the tall ice packs building up along the shore.

"You must like it out there," he said.

The waves broke high into the air, and the wind whipped the spray to mist.

"Do you remember those Canada trips we made with grandpa?" Jack said. "I remember once we were out on the lake and he thought he was snagged in the weeds. So we bring the boat over and he's not snagged at all. He has a monster bass on. Then later, as we were coming in, he swears he knows the light of the lodge. Dead sure. But when we get there we're about half a mile from where we should be. He was wrong twice that night."

"Your grandfather was wrong more than that in his life," his father said.

The fishing trips ended when Jack was still a boy and his mother died. At first, Jack didn't like the trips. Then later he wasn't sure. Sometimes now while fishing on the lake, he was quite sure he didn't like it at all.

He watched the play of firelight on the big crossbeam overhead. The old beams and siding made it seem dark inside, darker than it should.

"I didn't know you had a taste for whiskey." His father poured him another drink and handed back the glass.

"I don't, really," said Jack. He took two big gulps of the scotch, feeling the ice against his teeth and the hot liquor as it slid down to his stomach.

"I guess I never did till the army," his father said from the window.

For a moment, Jack saw the deer out in the bay before it disappeared again in the driving snow.

"Did you like the army?" he asked.

"I must have been about your age when they shipped me to the Pacific," his father said. "The guys I was with were a lot older than me. Hell-raisers, all of 'em. Why, we landed on enemy islands sometimes before the Marines did. We used to print buttons that read 'Welcome Ashore,' and then hand them out as they landed. Besides the air strips and quarters, they built some very fine bars. And that's about the time I acquired my taste for scotch, 1944, on the lovely island of Guam."

"Did you like it?" asked Jack. "The war, I mean."

"Oh, I had my times. I remember riding into the highlands at night in the jeeps, blasting hell out of dove. Once, a Japanese sniper hiding out in the jungle took a shot at us. Put a hole in the fender not two feet from my ass. But I was lucky, a lot luckier than being twenty inches from a slug in the butt. You're lucky there's not one on for you now."

"Sometimes I wish there was a war for me," said Jack.

"You don't know what you say."

"At least in war things are clear. You know what you have to do. At least you know."

"It's a waste," his father said. "It's time you could be getting on with things. A man only has to look after his own. That's it."

"I don't believe that."

"Believe it."

Jack stood up.

"I don't," he said. "It's got to mean something or it isn't worth it. I don't care what it is. If it doesn't mean anything, it's no good."

His father had that bemused look in his eyes again, that look of triumph.

Jack grabbed his coat and started for the door. "It's just got to," he said. "That's all."

Outside, the wind blew a long desolate howl. The whole landscape was as barren as he'd ever seen it. A scrub pine stood across the lane, stark and alone against the white. Beyond the snowed-in cabin he saw the contours of the ice piled on shore, the leaden sky, and the frozen bay where a buck struggled for his life. He knocked the logs together before stacking them in the barrel. He knew his father watched him from the window.

It was always the same with him. It didn't matter what was said just as long as he got him to take up the fight. It didn't matter how the words lined up. Many times he found himself arguing something he cared nothing about, but he cared nothing about most everything. With his father, he took up whatever was left over. He took up the other side. It was the fight that mattered, taking up the fight, and there was never any letting up. That's the way it had been for as long as he could remember. It might have all changed once, but it didn't.

He brought an armful of logs in and stacked four in the metal ring next to the fire. He put the last one in the flames. It made a hissing sound and beads of moisture bled on the wood.

"Let me tell you a story," his father said from the window. "I'm not exactly sure why it comes to mind just now, but it does. There's no moral to it, just remember that.

"After Guam they sent me to Hawaii to build quonset huts. Well, I didn't. I was in charge of Japanese prisoners, and they built them. It was the Navy's idea. Right from the beginning, you understand. Engineering school, the whole bit. I just did what they told me.

"Anyway, in Hawaii, there was this elderly Japanese prisoner. He was a professor in Tokyo before the war. He couldn't speak English very well so finally he just wrote down what he wanted to say. He wrote down the materials we needed and drew diagrams. I still have them. He organized all the prisoners and oversaw the work. He got them all to work, too.

"Once, we were alone and I showed him a picture of home. Then he showed me a picture of his family. So I show him a picture of your grandmother and grandfather. We're trading photographs like this when I realize I've leaned my rifle against the wall between us. It's as close to him as it is to me. He sees it too. He says something to me, but of course I can't understand him. So he takes the pencil and paper and writes, 'We are on one side and we are on two sides.' 'Friends and enemies,' he says. 'Always.' "

Jack watched his father take a long drink by the window.

"You have to understand, there was a war on. There were prisoners and I had my orders."

The deer was close now.

"He died, that old man. Took a bayonet in the heart from some jackass GI who couldn't find his cigarettes. Turns out they were under his bed the whole time."

The deer jumped three ice floes and gained the shore, stopping on the beach as a violent shudder raced through his body. With his balance back he bounded through the deep snow on the bluff. The last they saw of it, the deer was going for the woods.

"You should come out fishing again," said Jack.

But his father didn't move from the window. The light was fading, too. Outside, the light turned the blue of winter twilight that always came early.

Jack walked over and placed another log on the flames. For a moment, the fire flared up and cast a light across the room.

"It's getting late," he said.

It was always hardest now, with the light falling and all the things to do before dark. The day was all right and even the night. It was twilight that was hardest, with all the things to do at that time of the day.

JACK CLOSED THE DOOR behind him and walked outside into the cold evening. The bitter wind blew hard off the lake, straight out of the north. He broke away the ice that had gathered on the toboggan and cleared a path in front of the door with his foot. The wind swirled around the cabin from the lake, and he could see it now blowing across the big drifts in front of the woods. He stood and watched the wind blowing the snow in front of the trees in twilight.

They might not expect him down at the store. It was over a mile through the woods, and they might not be open when he got there. Pulling the toboggan behind him, Jack felt his eyes water over in the cold as he started out for the opening in the woods.

MORNING IN MAY

❖

On a morning in May, Jack looked out from his easy chair in the basement garage. Three canoes were stacked upside down in the grass by the docks. There was the faded red gas pump at the boat ramp. In the trees across the yard, a raven dropped from its perch and flew upriver. Logan was dead now, killed in early spring when his truck slid off the road and overturned in the river.

All three of the canoes needed repair. Two needed to be patched and the third had broken rivets where the bow piece attached to the gunwale. He'd opened the store at seven while Roni and the kids slept. Now, there was nothing to do until things picked up around noon. There was the fiberglassing, and maybe those ashes to bury from the trash barrels.

A boat was coming up the river, below the bridge. He could tell by the sound of the engine that it was his brother on his way to work.

Tom slowed the skiff at the bridge and let it coast upriver. He turned it in the current and revved it once for the ramp, cutting the engine as the boat slid up nicely next to the gas pump.

Jack poured a can of oil into the tank while his brother sat on the dock.

It was a quiet morning. The river was clear and copper in the sun. There were chickadees in the trees overhead and robins on the grass by the store. Upriver, the raven called once.

Jack switched on the pump and brought the nozzle to the tank. Kneeling down, he saw the minnow trap six feet deep in the river, in the hole at the bottom of the ramp where the boat motors blew out the sediment. A line ran from the cage up to a metal ring on the dock.

Logan had shown him how to rig the trap in the spring he and Roni bought the store. The ice had already broken in the river and together they set it up in the deep water. They built a holding tank out of the pine planks stacked under the trees behind the barrels. After Logan got him started, it was all Jack's show. He sold them by the dozen and made a fair go of it. This was in March, about the time the sap rises and the steelhead run, when every day the sun burns just a little warmer and the summer is close enough to feel in the air.

"Here," said Tom. "I'll take it."

Tom set the full tank in the back of the boat and reattached the line. He reached for the starter rope, then stopped and looked up.

"What," he said. "Am I supposed to pay now?"

Jack looked at the corrugated barn set back in the woods the way it always had been and the gas pumps by the cinderblock store, the birch trees where the truck pulled around and the tie stairway Logan had started last fall.

His brother handed him the money and Jack went up to the store for change. It was hot walking across the gravel lot and his legs felt heavy, weary.

When he returned with the half dollar, Tom was tying the skiff to a tree upriver. The raven called twice. His throaty squawks echoed down the corridor of trees, sounding both clear and faraway in the river air.

"I don't like that," said Tom, coming out of the woods.

"It's only a raven," said Jack.

"I still don't like it," his brother said.

Jack walked over to the docks and sat down by the river. The morning was quiet and still. Nothing moved at all. It wasn't strange that no one should be out this early in the morning. The rivet gun and fiberglass kit were on the dock next to him. They'd been there all morning. It was just that he didn't want to do the work yet.

The three canoes cast a long shadow over the grass, and as the shadow rolled back it left an edge of dew glistening in the sunlight. Rainbow starbursts winked along the edge until the heat proved too much and burned off the dew. A cricket's song faded beneath the canoes.

All the birds had gone quiet with the raven there. He couldn't see him, but Jack knew the raven waited around the bend. He called but there was no answer. He called again to the raven. Still nothing.

But he was up there all right, perched in some tree with the sun flashing off the black of his wing.

JACK STOOD UP AND raised the minnow trap from the bottom of the river. Air bubbles released from the screen and rose to the surface where they burst in the air. On the dock, he freed the live fish and threw the dead ones on the bank. He picked up the trap and reached down for the tools with the hand that held the half dollar. The half dollar. He didn't see his brother anywhere.

On his way to the three canoes, he turned the coin in his hand and flicked it into the river hole.

INCIDENT AT
THE MOUTH

❖

S ince early in the morning, campers, summer
people, and even a few locals came to the river for
the seven-mile canoe trip down to Lake Michigan.
They rented their canoes at the three liveries by the
bridge, then floated down to the river mouth and the
beaches at the big lake. There the workers loaded the
canoes onto trailers and returned them to the liveries
to be used again or placed in the woods alongside the
river. Only for a short while did *Logan's* run out of
canoes and its customers have to wait, as Jack and his
brother drove the black truck down to the mouth to
bring back as many as they could get. That was around

noon. Now, at least twenty canoes could be seen on the parking lot shore.

Jack pulled the trailer around and parked it by the river. There'd be six more loads after this one, but that was too far ahead to think. He collected the cushions and paddles while Tom dragged ten canoes up to the trailer. Together they loaded the canoes from the lowest rack up, swinging them into the slots with a controlled rhythm. After both sides were full, they hoisted the last two upside down on the cab and dropped them on stakes lodged in the truck bed. They strapped everything in and started back across the dusty lot.

On their way back to the store they passed the *Jenkins* jeep on the road, going down to the mouth. Jack waved, but this time Stan didn't wave back. They always waved to each other, no matter that Jenkins never got along with Logan. But none of the three storeowners got along that well, that's just the way it was. Jack and Stan were boyhood friends long before he went to work for Logan and Stan for his father. They fished together in the big lake and raced hydroplanes. One summer, they waterskied forty straight days and then only stopped because Stan's father needed him at the store. They traded skis once and decided both were the best. And though they no longer ran around together, they still talked across the river and waved to each other on the road. It was their own kind of pact. Their bosses might feud, but they would stay friends.

The truck coasted into the stop at the end of the road. Straight ahead, old man Jenkins leaned against one of his gas pumps.

"Jenkins didn't take kindly to us renting those canoes to *Waterside*," said Tom.

"How do you know?" asked Jack.

"Youngster said something about them blocking our canoes at the mouth."

The truck rumbled to a stop and now the old man was in clear sight. They could see the stubby cigar stuck in the corner of his mouth. They also saw that he watched them from under his greasy Evinrude cap.

"Oh, I'd give him a bit more credit than that, wouldn't you?" said Jack, turning onto the bridge.

Business was good for everybody and it didn't seem right that Jenkins should try something. Not today, Jack thought. But the feud ran deep between the two liveries across the river. There were times when Logan ran out of canoes and sent Jack down to the mouth to wait for any that came in. Instead of renting some from Jenkins at half price for his own customers, Logan made them wait. He rented canoes from *Waterside*, but never from Jenkins. For Logan to give Jenkins anything, no matter what, was simply unthinkable. It was understood that way. Jenkins was the same. Each spring the three owners got together and agreed on a single price for that summer. Jenkins advertised five dollars a canoe like the others but then he cut deals, especially when he could take business away from Logan. He always fought in the same roundabout way, never direct or upfront.

But it was different now. Now Logan was gone.

Jack backed the trailer down to the empty skeleton racks at the bottom of the yard. He and Tom moved the canoes one by one to the rack furthest back in the trees. Only once did he look across the river at the white docks in the glare of the sun. He didn't think about anything again until the last canoe was in the rack. He dropped it in the slot and rested a moment, knowing that part of the day's work was done, though it was only a small part.

Youngster pulled the truck and trailer around to the basement. He was younger than the two brothers and smaller. He jumped down from the driver's seat where he was met by Jack, stooped over and ready to spar.

"Get . . . get outta here, you . . ." he said, muttering an obscenity just loud enough to hear.

" 'You' *what*?" repeated Jack.

Youngster tried to wriggle along the side of the truck until Jack forced him to fight back. Youngster smacked the older boy on the sides of the head, then scrambled into the basement garage where he bombarded Jack with pebbles as he climbed into the truck bed. From the truck, Jack turned and whirled a cushion directly for his head. Youngster ducked just in time as the cushion slid across the concrete floor behind him.

"Ooooo, you sombitch!"

Jack and Tom laughed hard. Youngster seemed dazed by the near miss, repeating himself as he carried the cushions and paddles into the basement. Inside the garage, he and Tom stowed the paddles in a large barrel and hung the cushions up to dry in the rafters.

When he was finished in the truck, Jack jumped down and joined the other two in the shade. He took out a cigarette and passed around the pack.

"Jenkins got something up his sleeve, eh?" he said.

"I guess he's mad we rented those canoes to *Waterside* this morning when they run out," Youngster explained.

"So, we've done that before."

"Yeah, but maybe he thinks we made a deal with them," Youngster said. "Or maybe he just wants to see how far he can push us. Lately, I seen them build those canoe stacks. They're easier to load that way but they build 'em so nobody else can get to the beach, like they're the only ones that hasta pick up canoes. You know what I'm talking about."

Jack had seen the stacks of canoes before, but never so they blocked his way. But he knew that for all of Youngster's exaggerations, he didn't lie.

"I wouldn't be surprised if Jenkins got 'em building them things all over the parking lot by now," said Youngster. "And I betcha Stan's down there too, waiting for you. You know the old man. He likes to push."

A chorus of bird songs hung in the air outside, as the river flowed black beneath the cedar shadows upstream. A car hissed across the bridge.

"But all you gotta do is talk sense with him," Youngster said. "Stan don't want to get into it with you. You just have to let him know his old man's out of line."

Jack took a long last pull off his cigarette and looked at his brother. "Okay, you ready?"

Youngster jumped up. "Hey, you want me to come?"

"You better watch the pumps," said Jack. "Why don't you grab a few beers out of the ice machine, too."

Jack stood up and walked outside in the sunshine. He glanced across the river at the white docks, then looked into the trees on the other side. He studied two kingfishers quarreling about something before one flew upriver toward Big Platte Lake, its blue wings moving fast in the brilliant sky. He watched it as far as he could until it disappeared over the trees and he felt two cold bottles on his arm.

Tom backed the truck around and Jack hopped into the cab. He watched his brother shift the shaking stick to second gear, then work the gas and clutch until the big '72 Ford started to climb, slowly at first, the rear tires spinning a little in the gravel. The truck rumbled up the small rise to the asphalt lot and then onto the highway. Once across the bridge they turned down the river road, gaining speed past the campground.

Jack grabbed an opener out of the empty cans and wrappers on the floor. He applied it to the bottle caps slowly and deliberately to feel the muscles in his forearm working. He gave one of the bottles to his brother. The other he lifted to his mouth and held it there for a moment, feeling the sting in the back of his throat.

When the minister had spoken his peace and they started filling in the hole, Roni took him aside and told him that they would run the store just like always. People were stumbling away from the grave, crying and hanging onto each other, while Logan's widow told him that she would handle the store if he could run the show outside. Promise me, she said. It was as if she couldn't wait for the other business to get over with.

Jack gazed across the road at the sun flecks on the river surface and the play of shadow and light under the trees. The grass along the riverbank moved in the breeze, its lighter color showing when the wind got strong.

He didn't mind the long hours, the lifting, and even the people when they complained. It was all the rest—the talk, the hustlers and salesmen tipped off beforehand or just slick enough to catch wind they were dealing with somebody who couldn't even walk into a bar yet, when they started to lean on him and take advantage. It didn't take long to figure it all out.

As the road straightened out from the last curve, he watched the ripple of sky in the heat waves over the lake. Far out in the bay, fishing boats rolled up and down with the passing of each swell.

Jack looked across the lot where most of the canoes were beached. Stan and another worker stood next to two large stacks piled in front of the other canoes. From where they would have to park the truck, he and Tom could get a full load. But instead of pulling their canoes up to the trailer, they'd have to carry them one by one around the two piles of *Jenkins* canoes, a good forty feet out of the way.

"You only have to talk with him," his brother said.

"Just pull around and back up close," said Jack.

Tom turned the truck onto the lot and steered around the bend in front of Stan and the other worker. He pulled the truck ahead until the trailer came out of the turn, then backed it straight down for the canoes. When he had gone far enough, he came to a stop and cut the engine.

The two brothers stepped out of the truck. With the river beside them, Jack and Tom walked toward the two *Jenkins* boys.

Even when they got closer, Stan waited in that same patient way.

"Hiya, Jack," he said, as the wind swirled across the dusty lot. It blew from the west off the lake, then out the river mouth to the bay.

"Looks like the old man's got you busy," Jack replied.

The wind swept across the bay all the way to the dunes on the other side, erasing any tracks left behind in the sand.

"Be nice just to go carefree like the old days, huh Stan?"

"Those old days were trouble," Stan grinned. "I remember once or twice you getting us into trouble."

"There wasn't much we couldn't get away with back then, you and me," said Jack.

"You sure saw to it, all right."

"No one to tell us different, was there?"

Stan smiled and looked away. Downriver, the gulls and terns circled high above the mouth where the baitfish packed in. Whitecaps rolled off the lake.

"Guess that's the way it's always been," said Jack. "At least as long as I can remember."

"Yeah," said Stan. "Guess so."

"Guess before even you and me, huh?"

"Jack, we don't have to make a big deal of this."

Jack looked at his brother and the black truck with the bold white letters, the river mouth, and the dunes across the bay. He could hear the waves down on the beach.

"It's funny that way, isn't it?"

"Yeah," said Stan, no longer smiling. "It's funny, all right."

It took too long, the way he walked through the wind and the glare. The way he watched himself too at a distance, sealed off from what happened. It felt all right at first (It was not him, not *really* him) the way it always does (not him *now* in this place) with that first taste of blood the taste of copper and he let Stan hit him twice so everything jerked taut and clear, automatic, like he was awake for the first time seeing everything clear in the sun for the first time all day, for the first time in a long while.

They went around in a circle, stopping and starting, changing up one to the other. When he hit him, it made a popping sound like a knife when it first goes into the belly of a trout.

He hit him just like with Youngster, only now he could get it all out. He fought against the edgy feeling in his stomach and legs until Stan was bleeding too and tired. He fought against always having to watch out, against all the times there was someone there to push him some more, against the same thing day after day.

And he fought long after it seemed like a dream in the glare of the sun with the wind blowing out, long after he lost the feel of it.

"All right," said Stan finally, but Jack couldn't hear. Everything was falling . . . the sky, the dunes, all falling slowly down.

"All right," Stan said again, and dropped his hands.

Stan turned and motioned to the other boy. When he looked back, there was blood at the side of his mouth. He said something then, but Jack couldn't hear.

"Right, Jack?" he said again, grinning through the blood. "No hard feelings," Stan said.

WHILE THE OTHER BOY cleared the two pyramids of canoes, Jack went to the river and washed out the blood. He made sure to get it good and clean, to feel the cold water deep inside the cuts of his mouth.

His brother backed the truck down and together they loaded the canoes onto the trailer. There were a good twenty-five of them on the lot now with *LOGANS* stenciled on the sides. They tipped the canoes over until all the water poured out, then dragged ten up close. They put the paddles and cushions into the bed of the truck and loaded eight canoes on the trailer. The last two they loaded upside down on the back of the truck. He checked all the canoes for loose straps, then started toward the passenger door.

On his way to the truck, he noticed Stan looking on from the scattered canoes. He was standing by, just watching. There was nothing in the look that he gave him. Tom had the engine running. It was just like always, and he didn't think about a thing.

WRECK ON LOOKOUT HILL

❖

Youngster tossed him another beer from the front seat of the Mustang. Jack caught it from the hood of his Falcon and looked again at the boat cutting a V in the lake below.

"What'd you say was in here?"

Youngster's cousin was up from Detroit. He had the medium build and fair skin of Youngster but he was from the city, with neat hair. He came over and put a foot on the bumper.

"Straight six," said Jack. "Nothing fancy."

The boat followed the near shoreline, but it was too far away to hear the engine. Jack liked watching all the boats from this distance. The quiet made everything seem different. He liked the rooster-tails from waterskiers when the spray flashed in the sun, and the shadows of wind as they moved across the water.

"My Mustang has a four twenty-nine, hemi-head," said the cousin.

Through a break in the trees, Jack could see all of Glen Lake below. At the far end of the lake, the dune country rolled back to Lake Michigan. He liked it best in late afternoon when the air over the dunes was hazy and sundrenched and he couldn't tell where the dunes ended and the sky began. It was a good place to be by yourself and have the world at a distance, to be alone and above everything.

"I race down in Detroit, you know."

The speedboat raced up the shoreline, but he couldn't hear it.

"All over the state," said the cousin, "but Detroit's the best."

"Uh huh," mumbled Jack.

The boat veered around a point and disappeared, leaving a trail of wake that faded out across the turquoise water.

Youngster sat in the bucket seat with the door open.

"And what are you going to ride when you get old enough?" asked Jack. "Let me guess, a pickup."

"That's right," Youngster replied in his best northern drawl.

"How are we going to cruise all the backroads in a bouncy old pickup? How are we going to cover the county like that?"

But Youngster was no longer listening, watching his cousin instead. "We're all out of beer," he said.

"Maybe we ought to hit that party store down at the bottom."

Jack slid off the hood and started for the front seat of his car.

"You going to show us what this old Falcon has?" the cousin smiled.

"Not on this road," Youngster warned.

The cousin stepped into the driver's seat with his crooked smile.

Jack looked in his mirror and saw the red Mustang all waxed and shiny. When it went by he couldn't help noticing the chrome wheels, how they were so clean and perfect in the swirling dust. A fuzzy ornament swung from the mirror. Racing stripes ran up the sides. He noticed everything as it coasted up to the blacktop. When the brake lights flashed red, he power-shifted past the Mustang in a whirl of dirt and squealing tires.

Jack ran the Falcon through the gears and looked back. The Mustang followed right behind on a short straightaway. He entered the first turn high then dropped low so the tires clung to the berm. The road was old and worn smooth with no shoulder, only sand for a few feet before the start of the woods. The road snaked the other way and he steered through the oncoming lane into another, longer straightaway. The Mustang was nowhere in sight. Jack touched the accelerator and the Falcon lunged again. But he was going too fast. The road dropped even steeper before the next turn, the last turn on the hill, the one that hairpinned more than ninety degrees. But he was too far into it to brake. He gripped the wheel and muscled it around, careful not to look at the centerline too closely. If he cut too much he might lose it right then, but if he drifted too wide he would surely spin out trying to get back into the turn. His arms locked on the wheel but the road kept bending until he was losing control and the car started to slide. When his rear tire hit the sand, he pulled the emergency brake and held on.

WHEN IT ALL STOPPED, everything was on its side. He was somewhere in the woods. He tried the door but it was too heavy. The car was on its side somewhere in the woods.

He pushed himself up and pulled the handle, extending an arm to keep the door open. When he jumped, the metal edge of the door nicked him on the head and he felt the warm blood in his hand.

Through a break in the woods, he saw the rusted cable of an old guard-rail by the road. His Falcon had gone over the edge somehow and crashed in the trees. He scrambled through the broken woods up to the road where Youngster and his cousin were running down to meet him. There were people coming up from the other direction.

"You all right?!" cried Youngster. "Man, I thought you was dead. I told my cousin, 'He's dead!' "

Through the trees, Jack could see the big summer cottages at the bottom of the hill. There were people standing around he didn't know. Uphill from the guard-rail, a broken telephone pole hung sideways in the trees.

"You must have hit the pole and swung around here." Youngster pointed to the space of sand between the telephone pole and guard-rail. Further down, the Falcon tilted nose-first in the trees. "You sure you're all right?"

He was dazed not so much from the accident as from the strangeness of things, the people and all the noise. When he first heard the man it seemed like just another voice in the strange noise. He didn't know what he said, but something made him turn around. Then the noise went away and all he saw was the threat. The anger and the threat. Then the hard shove in the chest and the reflex to stay on his feet. The man from one of the summer cottages came at him again. They struggled to the ground, half on the road and half in the sand, until Jack swung his weight around and pinned the man's face to the asphalt with his elbow. All around him he heard the voices of people he didn't know. The man was older than him, old enough to be his father. But this was something he had done a hundred times before with Youngster, with his brother. He heard the strange voices closing in and he dug the elbow harder. He could see the anger leaving the man's face. He dug harder still with the threats and accusing voices closing in on the edge, with less and less resistance. Someone screamed and the face twisted against the road, the smooth macadam road, when it all went under in a flash of electric white.

"YOU THERE, JACK?"

Youngster was standing over him on the side of the road.

"I had to do it, you know," he said.

His face and white hair looked strange against the blank sky.

"Sheriff's gone now, but he called an ambulance. You don't need any help, do you?"

Jack sat up and felt the bump on his head, the sharp splitting pain in his head. They were alone on the road.

"What happened?"

"You lost control," said Youngster, showing him the jack iron. "So I took you out."

The woods were darker now. The sky was white.

"With the *jack*?"

"Yeah, the jack."

Youngster helped him up and together they walked over to the Falcon. A wrecker had winched it out of the woods up to the road. There was a large dent in the side from the telephone pole and smaller dents all the way around.

Jack stepped into the driver's seat and started it right away. The Mustang pulled alongside, and he told Youngster that he could make it back without them.

He followed the Mustang until he lost sight of its red taillights, then pulled off the road. Underneath the car he saw the broken emergency cable dangling down to the ground. That explains the dragging noise, he thought, but not the hissing. He opened the hood and found the steady stream of water from the gash in the radiator. He drove a couple miles further until the temperature gauge read hot, then parked the car for good in the dusty lot of a fruit stand.

The sun had long since fallen over the bluff in the west when he started walking down the road. It was ten miles back by road, but only seven or so if he cut through the dunes. On the other side of town he could pick up the trail leading down to the beach. He could take the trail through the dunes, down to the creek.

Jack walked over to the side of the road and stepped through the wire fence at the edge of the or-chard. He picked a handful of cherries and wiped them on his shirt. They were the sour kind and still a little yellow around the stem. The juice cut through the dryness, and it stung where he was bleeding. The trees grew in straight lines and he walked in until he was far enough away from the road and the trees made a good cover. He found a soft clearing with an opening to the sky where the fruit trees closed in around him. He sat down and looked up at the stars in the deep blue sky, closing his eyes with the hot restless feeling inside, trying to let it slip away.

He should have known that turn was coming. That was his hill, his road. He should have braked sooner, but he knew that. He'd been down that hill a hundred times. He knew that road and still he went faster when he was going too fast already. But he had to go that fast, he knew that now. He always had to go faster. And that man, angry because he was going too fast. He should have known. That man should have known not to come after him like that. He could have killed that man, kept going and driven his head right into the road. The man should have known you don't go that far. Should have seen it in his eyes, you don't come that close. He'd have died a little right there and next time it would be a whole lot easier. You can only go so far. He knew this as much as he knew anything, if he could know anything at all, and that was all he knew.

And with the stars coming out one by one in the break of the trees, he breathed harder still until he couldn't stand it any longer and had to keep walking.

He walked along the shadows at the edge of the orchard, all the way to town. It was hardly big enough to call a town but he walked the backstreets anyway, past the lawns and dark windows of the white clapboard houses. At the edge of town he cut through the last orchard, finding his way among the cherry trees until he came out on a hill overlooking the village. At the bottom of the orchard, a light shone across an old tractor parked in the weeds. Somewhere in the distance, beyond the last circle of soft yellow light, a dog barked up at him.

Jack hiked to the top of the bluff and left it all behind him in the open dune country. Dead ghost trees stood twisted and bare in the dunes along the ridge. There were no other footprints and he could see the windrows that had formed in the sand. He walked across the dune to the other side where the open bluff dropped down to a darkness above the lake. Jack traversed the bluff, slowly at first, making deep footprints in the sand. He cut a sharper path down the hill, feeling the darkness over the lake. He went faster still in bigger strides, careening off the face of the bluff until it seemed he could almost take off and fly. And forever it seemed like the lake reached out in an endless desire under the stars.

He ran all the way down until he heard the waves on the beach, and the sound of the running creek where it came out between the trees. The woods were dark where the creek came down to the lake. Jack walked out to the middle and let his feet sink deep into the picture of stones beneath the current. He fell to his knees and crawled up to where the water was smooth under the trees and he could see his reflection on the surface with the stars and sky above. In the darkness of the trees, he went under and breathed in the creek. Fighting back the shock, he stayed until everything blurred and he was everywhere numb, and for a long time there was nothing but the strange feeling of floating.

When he came out, it hurt badly and he dragged himself through the sand. He looked out from the sand, with the stars and shadows forming again . . . the edge of everything coming back again.

A TROUT ROSE
ON THE RIVER

A trout rose on the river. The rings spread from the point of action, fading on the surface as they drifted down with the current through the moon's reflection. A trout rose on the river, then another, and the rings overlapped.

These were small trout, not like the browns that came in to feed along the shore of Lake Michigan. As a boy, he had watched and waited for the schools of brown trout that came in to feed along the sandbar. He watched for the ripples on the surface when the lake was calm, then waded out for the trout that always kept a distance. Sometimes one broke free from the school and swam up close to him on the sandbar. The trout swam close but always a gentle thrust of the tail kept it away. He might reach again, but always the trout kept a distance. He'd watch until the fish was gone and nothing remained but the reflection on the surface of the two islands and the big dune to the north.

He knew about the legend as a boy, the story of the bears and the sand dune. He waited until everything was right, then started out one morning for the other side of the bay. For hours he saw nothing in the fog but the circle of flat water around his canoe. The water was clear and glassy and he could see deep into the lake. When he got to the other side he saw the line of pilings from the old lumber camp. They were down below the surface, rising out of the darkness under his canoe as he drifted past in the fog, the pilings from the old lumber camp vanished long ago.

There were no schools of trout along the sandbar. There hadn'ta been for a while, and he got into his car. Tonight, the lake was calm and the smell drifted in like a bad wind. Flies swarmed on the rotting alewives down on the beach. Looking out the window of his cabin he could hear the flies, what the low drone of black flies sounded like on the beach. He drove his Falcon down to the boat ramp at the mouth of the river but there was no one there, no Indian waiting with a winch on his bow, no scared-off poacher skulking around.

He got back in the car and drove all the way out past the cherry orchards to the woods at the county line. He turned onto a fire road and followed it to the end. Once these were virgin woods with big maple and hemlock towering in the sky. There was space in the woods, then. There was space enough to look straight up to the tops of the trees.

The road ended at a tumbledown shack on the edge of an oldfield meadow. The grass in the meadow was high and dead and it broke under his feet. Through a splintered window frame he saw glass shards and old newspapers scattered on the floor, broken chair legs, and animal scat.

Two old cars sat in the grass behind the shack. One was a black Packard and he looked in at the steering wheel and oversized numbers on the gauges in the dash. The car sat low in the grass. Ferns grew in front where the engine used to be. Only one door remained, on the passenger side, and it was shot up nicely with a dozen bullet holes.

On the outside of the car, he followed the rusted edge of the body down into the ground. The rust and dirt were working toward the same color and he thought back to the days of gangsters, the outlaws who by their own wits could escape and hide out in a place like this. He thought of the house all in order and the hats and vests they wore then. He could see the cars too, with the shiny chrome and whitewalls. And the days, the long warm days spent in the woods with the red-tailed hawks circling overhead. The thinking, the planning, and finally the morning when the cars rolled down the road, the two of them moving steadily, leaving a trail of dust that hovered a while after they disappeared into the trees.

He turned and walked back through the woods past the outhouse, away from the shanty and Packard. He got into his car and drove steadily out to the main road, and the tamarack bog where Melissa Hayes lived.

Melissa Hayes lived in a trailer with her Indian mother at the edge of a bog called Deadstream. There were grand stories of watersnakes, big northern watersnakes in Deadstream, though he had never seen any. Their trailer sat on cinder blocks at the end of a narrow two-track, flanked on one side by a propane tank and a rusty trash barrel.

Melissa came out and together they drove down to the river where they sat for a long time in silence. They were far away from anyone now, deep in the woods at the bottom of a two-track where the river came around a stand of cedar. Many times they came here to drink. They went to other places—Otter Creek, Point Betsie, the mouth—but mostly they came here. There was nothing else to do. They came here to drink and to watch the river.

Melissa turned to him and smiled in the green light of the radio. The shadow from her hair fell across her face, her high cheekbones and dark eyes. In the green light of the radio he looked down her neck, down to where her shirt ended to the tight fit of her jeans. The night came on slowly this time of year. It came on slowly under the light of a half moon. All the edges so sharp in daytime blurred now. Shadows blended and moved. The air was warm and smelled of the river. There were owls in these woods and bobcat. There were bullfrogs and crickets nearby, and sometimes their long steady drone stopped dead.

A trout rose on the river, the rings drifting down through the moonlight on the surface.

"There's another gillnet in the bay," he said.

They were close together in the car. They had been like that for some time, close together watching the river in the dark glow of the night.

"Someone just left it."

The radio played an old song and he could tell by the sound of it that it came across the lake.

"So what are you going to do?" Melissa sigh

It came from the west like the winds, west like the bears.

"About your gillnetters and trout. About the people, Jack Young . . . ."

In the legend, the bears came east across the lake. They were driven to the western shore by the great fires and they looked across to the other side. And when they swam across the lake, the mother looked behind her for her two cubs. When she reached the other side, she climbed a hill and looked back to see her two cubs in the lake, first one then the other. She looked back for her cubs and saw the two islands, first one and then the other. And when she saw the islands where her cubs had been, she lay on the hill and went to sleep forever. The wind blew the sand where she lay. The wind blew and covered her with sand where she lay on the hill and slept forever.

"The people," she whispered. "The people who see you getting around with my mother's halfblood daughter."

Her long black hair brushed against his ear. They came down to the river.

"To hell with them," he said.

"To hell with them, too," she whispered.

"To hell with the whole show."

"To hell with the whole show, too."

"And to hell with the hell of it."

"That too."

Melissa pulled herself closer. She put her cheek against his and tightened the fingers on his leg.

"Let's go in," she said.

In the dark, he saw her skin.

"In the river."

A trout rose on the river and then another, the rings spreading, drifting, overlapping.

He saw her in the dark pull him under, her long black hair around her, pull him under to the bottom. He saw her in the dark, her face and all around her her long black hair in the dark.

END OF SUMMER

❖

Jack flicked a switch and the inside lights went out. Nobody was on the bridge tonight outside the store.

The river flowed silently along the cedar banks downstream, disappearing in a flat expanse of woods silhouetted against the sky.

There were always people on the bridge this time of night, campers mostly, leaning on the rail looking down at the river. Sometimes there was a girl, a stranger waiting alone with nothing around but the splash of streetlight on the other side, and he'd take her down by the river or through the dark smoky campgrounds to some sandy place back in the woods.

He flicked two switches but the outside lights stayed on. The campgrounds were empty now, summer was over. It used to be he couldn't wait until they were gone.

He flicked another two and nothing happened.

"Dammit," he said, looking to the switches he needed, the ones he knew by heart, and snapped off the yellow light.

Jack went down to the basement and closed the sliding garage door. He jammed the butt of a broken canoe paddle behind the wheel track and hurried back upstairs. His brother and Youngster would know now that he was closing.

He locked the cash register and returned to the window by the breaker panel. The bridge was still empty. Across the river, the streetlight had come on. He dead-bolted the front door and shut off the last light.

Outside in the dark, he saw his brother walking across the gravel yard.

"Tom."

"Is that you, Jack?"

"Lock the barn," he said. "Did Youngster get the cooler like I told his young ass? Where is he, anyhow?"

"We're closing pretty early, aren't we?"

Jack had the keys in his hand and spun them once around the ring. "Let's just get out of here," he said.

The two brothers walked down to the jeep parked in the trees along the river. The day before, Jack painted LOGANS over the fenders and now he could see the big white letters in the dark. From the other direction, the dim figure of a white-haired skinny kid struggled with a styrofoam cooler.

"I got it," said Youngster, sliding the squeaking cooler in back. He climbed up and took a seat behind Jack.

They drove the jeep a mile north on the highway before turning onto a dirt road leading down to Lake Michigan. In the clearing above the trees they could see the first stars of night shining in the sky. Jack drove fast down the dirt road, steering around the washboards and flooded-out potholes. Once, coming around a corner, the jeep started to slide and he had to correct the steering. He looked up and saw Youngster in the mirror, holding on by the roll bar.

Instead of taking the long left turn to the lake, Jack veered off at a two-track that headed north into the woods. He let the jeep roll all the way to a stop before reaching back and grabbing a can of beer out of the cooler. He watched as Youngster brought out two more cans and opened one up for himself.

"Go easy," said Jack. "It burns a little."

Youngster took a long drink of the beer and winced. "It tastes awful."

Jack laughed and popped the metal ring on his can. "You grow into it, I guess," he said.

Above the trees, the early stars blinked in a violet sky.

"This trail goes all the way to Otter Creek, doesn't it?"

"Yep," replied Youngster. "You have to make a turn or two, but it'll get you there."

"Maybe we shouldn't take it off the road," Tom said.

It had been a hard summer for all of them. With Logan gone, they ran the canoe livery while Roni kept the store and handled the paper work and creditors. Sometimes at night, Jack saw the strain in the young widow's eyes as if one more little thing might break her for good. But it never happened, and as the summer wore on he saw how she changed too. The jeep was hers. She'd bought it used with the insurance money.

Jack continued down the two-track, steering around the potholes and pine roots. The woods were darker now in the fading light. A half-mile in, they came to a thick post in the middle of the trail. Jack stopped the truck and they all got out to look.

"The park must have done it," said Youngster.

"The *National Park*?"

"Yeah," he said. "I seen a truck of theirs lately. They're starting to move in."

Jack grabbed the post at the base, but it barely moved. He took a step back and looked at his brother. "Give me a hand?"

Tom walked over and together they pulled the post out of the sand. Youngster laughed wildly as the brothers counted to three and heaved the post as far as they could into the ferns. They turned back toward the jeep when Youngster suddenly stopped.

"Look!"

Behind them on the trail, the headlights of a truck knifed up and down through the woods. The three boys scrambled into the jeep and sped away, barely missing a thick pine tree.

"Take a left!" cried Youngster, pointing down the trail. One way went south to two ponds and Otter Creek. The other way angled north to Deer Cabin and the dunes.

Jack turned off at the fork and followed the two-track behind a thick cover of sumac. He cut the lights, slid the transfer gear to four-high, and looked back.

Just when it seemed the Park truck had turned the other way, its headlights cut sharply down the trail in their direction.

Jack cried out laughing as they drove away into the night. He went fast down the trail, sliding through the curves and sand patches. The puddles got longer, deeper. Sometimes the wipers couldn't clear the windshield fast enough and he had to drive blindly with the wheel straight, hoping the trail didn't suddenly turn on them.

At Deer Cabin, Youngster pointed to a narrow passage cutting through the woods. Jack steered down the trail through the last of the trees when a whole new wild land opened up. Dune grass and juniper draped the rolling landscape. Lone pine trees stood atop the highest knolls, twisted toward the southeast like the crooked masts of shipwrecks. Youngster rose out of his seat and howled in delight, his long albino hair blowing out behind. It was all wild country for as far as they could see, with the big dune up the coast and the two islands across the bay. Whitecaps rolled across the lake, and a dark fiery light burned in the west.

"Hey, we shook him good!" Youngster laughed.

"Yeah, we did. This thing goes all right!"

Jack drove off the high dunes and stopped where they could see it all.

"What if he comes after us?" Tom said. "He can always find our tracks."

"He's not going to come out here," said Jack, wanting to get his brother on his side. "Not tonight."

"Man," said Youngster. "Roni'd kill us if she knew where her jeep was right now."

They paused, and then all three broke up laughing. The minute Jack saw the post there in the middle of the two-track, he felt that old fire inside and for awhile everything came clear again. It was just him and the ranger, everything out in the open where he could see it. It would have been all right the other way, too, he would have known what to do. But he slipped him and now it was good to hear his brother laugh. He slipped him in the new jeep and now they were out on the dunes. They were in the free, and all he could think of was that any feeling he had going for him was lost when the ranger missed that turn.

"Hey, what about the sand bowl?"

It was the same thing staring out the window to-night, hitting every switch but the one he needed. Just like he needed to have that old feeling back again, he needed to have somebody on the bridge, too. But the bridge was empty and it looked eerie in the faint light of dusk, the way a deer skeleton looks deep in the woods at night. . .

"Hey, Jack."

. . . and the river down underneath, the river the whole time flowing green-black for that space of dark woods. . . . .

"Jack," said Youngster.

"What?"

"The sand bowl. Do you want to try for the sand bowl?"

There were two bowls to the north. They could get there by following the bluff above the beach.

"We're right there, practically."

Jack waited for his brother. It was a long way off, more than what Youngster was making it out to be.

"I don't know," said Tom. "What about Roni? What if we get stuck?"

"Forget it," said Jack, putting the jeep in gear. "Let's just go."

"Yeah!" exclaimed Youngster from the back. One of his front teeth jutted out further than the rest and it caught on his lip.

They followed an old jeep trail north, banking one way then the other between dunes. The further they went the less they saw of it until the trail disappeared altogether and they followed along by the contour of the bluff. Jack kept a steady speed in low gear, careful to keep the momentum up when they climbed a hill and backing off some when they lurched downward.

They could see the first bowl at the end of the headlights in the distance. Driftwood posts marked an old dune buggy course that nobody had been on in years. Dune grass and shifting sand had obscured the last of the tire grooves long ago.

Jack accelerated up the last ascent.

The driftwood posts loomed in a black sky. Ghost shadows crawled across the sand when something happened. He thought it slipped out of gear, but the lever was in place. The engine still idled and he gunned it again. He shifted gears and pulled on the transfer stick, shifting and revving, but the jeep wouldn't move.

"The wheels in back aren't spinning!"

He saw Youngster's face in the mirror, lit up in the glow of headlights, and he revved it harder. He could hear echoes from the engine racing back and forth across the dunes. He tried it again, but the jeep still didn't move.

Finally he jumped down and looked underneath. "Try it somebody!"

His brother set it in gear and released the clutch. The front wheels spun in the sand, lifting two white veils that fell when the engine idled.

But there was nothing from the back. The universal was shot.

Jack closed his eyes and saw Youngster's pale face again in the creeping shadows of headlights. Somebody cut the engine and he looked at the dark underside of the jeep, the universal, and the plain of dune grass stretching down to the beach, all the fingers of grass reaching up in the wind.

THEY SAT FOR A long time listening to the wind and the sound of the waves breaking on the beach. There were no bonfires along the coast tonight, no headlights at the end of the lake road. Below them, the jeep sat dark and muted at the bottom of the sand bowl.

"Hey look, there's a light."

It was behind them to the southeast, in the highest trees. Tom stood up and walked to the top of the dune.

"It's the moon," he said, coming back. "It's just the moon coming up over the ridge."

"Oh," said Youngster, drinking his beer.

From where they sat, Jack could see the bluffs along the coast and the two islands across the bay. Behind him, the dunes rolled back to a dark edge of woods cut against the sky. Whitecaps broke along the beach, and in the west a streak of blood red light still burned on the horizon. The last glimpse of day, he thought.

The end of summer.

"I know of a cabin up the creek a ways," said Youngster. "I could sneak back for my gun and we could hide out there. Leave the store behind. Leave everything behind."

Jack could see the dock pilings from the old logging town where the creek emptied in. They were all that remained of the ghost town. They stood in a line out to the deep water where they trailed off to nothing in the darkness under the lake.

"That's right. You're seventeen now, aren't you Jack? Why hell, they can throw you in jail."

He could feel it getting cold. He could hear it in the kid's voice. There'd be a thick fog over the river by now. The water would be just like glass back in the woods.

"I used to hunt up the creek over there," said Youngster finally. "There's an old trail that leads into the woods. One time up by the pond, I flushed out a big ole black bear."

Youngster's white hair fairly glowed in the dark. It was always hard on him because of what he was, because he looked different. It made him see things a different way. He drew a circle in the sand with his beer can and looked straight at Jack.

"It chased me, too," he said. "Chased me down the creek till I turned around and shot it through the ear."

THE WIND SWEPT ACROSS the dunes, all the way back to the bluffs on the ridge. A white moon rose over the trees in the south. With the stars overhead they sat and waited in the dark, listening to the waves as they rolled in off the lake, one after the other.

When all the beer was gone they started back along the trail. They kept to the jeep tracks, walking in the tire lines above the beach. The pace was a little quick for Youngster, but he kept up with the two brothers.

A freighter had come around the point heading north across the lake. The ship was lit from bow to stern with bright deck lights, brighter than the stars even. Out there on the horizon, the lights burned like the fourth of July.